Captain Rosalie

For Jeanne
T. F.

To Molie, the biggest of little readers I know
I. A.

For Sarah, Simon, and Gabriel
S. G.

Text copyright © 2014 by Timothée de Fombelle
English translation copyright © 2014, 2018 by Walker Books Ltd.
Illustrations copyright © 2018 by Isabelle Arsenault

First U.S. edition 2019
This story previously appeared, in slightly different form, in *The Great War* (Candlewick Press, 2015)

Library of Congress Catalog Card Number pending

ISBN 978-1-5362-0520-6

18 19 20 21 22 23 24 APS 10 9 8 7 6 5 4 3 2 1

Printed in Humen, Dongguan, China

This book was typeset in New Clarendon.
The illustrations were done in watercolor, pencil, and ink.

Candlewick Press
99 Dover Street
Somerville, Massachusetts 02144

visit us at www.candlewick.com

TIMOTHÉE DE FOMBELLE

Captain Rosalie

illustrated by

ISABELLE ARSENAULT

translated by Sam Gordon

CANDLEWICK PRESS

I have a secret.

The others think I'm drawing in my notebook when I'm sitting on the little bench underneath the coat hooks at the back of the classroom. They think I'm dreaming as I wait for evening to fall. And the teacher passes me by as he gives instruction to the students.

He places his hand on my hair.

But I am a soldier on a mission. I am spying on the enemy. I am preparing my plan.

I am Captain Rosalie.

I'm disguised as a little girl, five and a half years old, with my shoes, my dress, and my red hair. To go unnoticed, I don't wear a helmet or a uniform. I stay there, silent. A far as the other children are concerned, I'm the little girl who comes and sits at the back of the room and does nothing all day long.

My mother has worked at the factory since the start of the war, ever since my father went off to fight. Now I'm too old to go to the nanny's, so every morning my mother drops me beneath the sheltered part of the yard at the school for the older children, before the sun is even up.

The school yard is deserted. I wait all by myself, eating the bread and butter that my mother has knotted into one of my father's big handkerchiefs. Dogs bark in the distance, out there by the farms. The dead leaves whistle their way across the school yard.

The teacher arrives at seven o'clock in the morning. Since coming back from the war, he has only one arm. But he smiles as though having just the one is quite something. That and being here in the silence of the school.

"Still at your post, young lady?"

He should be calling me "Captain" and saluting, but I keep quiet. Secret mission. I can't give anything away.

The teacher said to my mother at the start of the year that he would look after me, that he would let me sit at the back of the older children's classroom and do my drawing, that he would give me a notebook and some pencils.

My mother shook his hand for a very long time to show her thanks.

I hold his large bag in my lap while he opens up the school. His belongings carry the aromas of woodsmoke and coffee. This must be what it smells like in his brightly lit house just behind the school.

One of the older children, Edgar, arrives before the others, because he's always in trouble and has to light the stove in the classroom as punishment. I like Edgar a lot. I can see that he doesn't listen to a thing, that he simply won't learn how to count or read, but one day I will make him a lieutenant. Edgar lets me strike the match before throwing it into the stove. The fire, when it gets going, is the same color as my hair, like a little brother who looks like me.

4

When the students arrive, I am already sitting down at the back of the room in my place against the wall. They are two or three years older than me. I let myself be covered by the coats as they hang them above my head without paying any attention to me. I wait a bit, and when they are all at their desks, with their backs to me, I push the coats aside as if I were bursting from the undergrowth and ambushing them from behind in a clearing.

Only Edgar notices me, with my notebook gripped in my hand.

But I'm already listening to the teacher, who is reading aloud from the first page of the newspaper. Every morning he gives us news of the war.

"Yesterday, Tuesday, the German troops were crushed at the Somme. Our men are fighting and reporting victories." Then he says, "We must have faith."

And then some mysterious names: Combles, Thiepval . . . recaptured villages.

The teacher always gives us good news, never bad. He leaves the students standing behind their chairs a little longer, in silence. He tells them that they must think of our soldiers who are giving up their youth, their lives. Sometimes, when he speaks like that, I get the feeling that he is looking at me, and I turn away so as not to catch his eye. How could he know about my mission?

When at last the class sits down, I pretend to be

elsewhere, lost in my thoughts, even though I am

concentrating perfectly. I am Captain Rosalie, and I have

infiltrated their squad this fall morning in 1917.

I know what I have to do. One day I'll be awarded a

medal for this. It's already gleaming deep within me.

The freckles beneath my eyes, the animals I draw on

the page, the long socks up to my knees . . . all that

is just camouflage. I have heard that soldiers hide with

bracken sewn into their uniforms. My ferns are the scabs

on my knees, the vacant daydreaming, the tunes I hum—

sweet little melodies for a sweet little girl.

The teacher writes symbols on the blackboard, and the

students read them out loud. I watch the boy in the first

row as he stands up and approaches the board.

He writes some other mystical signs. He never makes a mistake. His name is Robert, the gendarme's son. The teacher congratulates him and sends him back to his desk. I keep a close eye on Robert. I know how important it is to spot the best soldiers and learn their secrets.

The teacher whispers as he passes close by me.

"Go and get some coal, Rosalie. That'll keep you busy."

I stand up from my bench. The coal is stored outside, behind the classroom, beneath the window. I cannot show that I don't want to be away.

"You can leave your book."

But I keep it in my hand. Never let the enemy seize your weapons. As soon as I reach the door,

I run through the cold toward the pile of coal.

I have to get back quickly. I must not abandon my post.

In the evenings, my mother comes to pick me up from
the empty school. The teacher and the students have long
since left. She squeezes me in her arms and rubs her head
against mine. Lucky I'm not wearing my helmet.
I breathe in the scent of her hair, which smells good.

   "I've missed you, Rosalie."

She is very tired, and I love this tiredness. I love it when courage deserts her and her eyes are red. But very quickly she composes herself and takes my hand.

"Look!"

She takes an envelope out of her pocket. I recognize these white envelopes, covered in postmarks and black and red stamps. It's a letter from my father.

"Come, Rosalie. I'll read it to you."

As she pulls me along by my hand, no one can see anything on my face. I show nothing of my thoughts. I feel my mother's fingers clinging hard to my ink-stained hand.

"When I get home, I'm going to take Rosalie fishing."

Lying on my bed, I look at my mother from the side, the letter perched in her lap.

"I thought about the stream below the mill. I saw some trout leaping there before the war. Rosalie will learn to swim. Do you have that recipe for trout with walnuts? Can you be sure that there are some walnuts left for it if I come home in the spring?"

I close my eyes. I don't like all this stuff. My mother keeps reading.

"My darling, I am thinking of you. I know that Rosalie

is a good girl. And that the teacher is happy to have her

and help her. And as for you, I know your work is tiring.

You'd like to spend more time with your little girl. But

every time I load a shell into the cannon, I say to myself

that maybe it was you who made it at the factory. It's like

you are at my side in battle. Yes, the women are helping

us by working so hard in the factories, and the children

keep us going by lending their mothers support and being

good."

I try not to listen. Anyway, I couldn't care less about

being good. I don't lend my mother to anyone. I don't

want to hear any talk of fish leaping in streams. I don't

believe in stories of walnuts and mills.

Not one memory other than war. I was too young before it.

And I can see that my mother is still reading, for a long time, although there is just a single page of writing in the envelope. I can see that she continues even when the candle stops flickering in the bedroom.

She shows me a drawing on the back of the sheet of paper, lines of charcoal depicting a landscape. It's the only thing that seems true. A forest in the distance and the land in the foreground all churned up, with soldiers hiding in holes. I recognize my father's way of drawing. I have seen him three times when he's been home on leave to have a rest from the war. He hardly spoke, but he held me tight in his arms and he drew horses in the mist on the window.

I fall asleep thinking of horses streaming across the glass.

In bed, I dream of a medal being attached to my nightgown. I dream of a general placing his hand on my shoulder. I feel the coldness of the medal against my skin.

Each day, my mission continues its advance. Each day I, Captain Rosalie, am at my post at the back of the class, ready for a surprise attack beneath the coats.

I look at the inscriptions on the blackboard as if they form a battle plan. I try to remember everything. I copy little bits down in the back pages of my notebook. No one pays me any attention. The older children have forgotten about me. I have become a gray coat hooked amid the others. Only the teacher remembers me from time to time. And Edgar, the dunce, my lieutenant, who throws curious looks my way. I feel he is waiting for his time to come.

In the evening, my mother comes to pick me up. Sometimes she has a new letter in her pocket, sometimes not. Just that beckoning to take me into her arms, those eyes that never leave mine. I prefer this to all that talk about the trout we are going to fish for, about swimming in the stream or the jams we will make one day after picking wild raspberries. The letters stay in the toffee box, on top of the shelves in the kitchen. They're better up there.

The weeks are very alike. Sometimes, at night, I open my window and lean out to listen. To listen carefully. I wonder if I might hear the noise of the war, way off in the distance, beyond the dogs at the farms.

And then one day, on my birthday, I am given snow.
Snow up to above my ankles. I can barely open the
door in the morning. I let out a cry. Flakes are falling all
around.

My mother doesn't go to the factory that day because
it is snowing too heavily. I stay with her at home. This is
surely the greatest day of my life. We play hide-and-seek in
the house. She doesn't even get dressed. I find her curled up
in bed, still wearing her nightgown. She startles me. I forget
about Captain Rosalie. I almost forget about my father.

My mother rolls me up in a blanket, laughing. Since
there is nothing to eat and we cannot go out, we drink
milk sweetened with sugar. We snuggle together in the
armchair opposite the fireplace.

I watch the redheaded flames as they dance. Then
my mother climbs up to get the big cloth on top of the
wardrobe. She takes out her wedding dress. She shows
me that it still fits her.

"It's just a little tight here—look."

She laughs again. Before nightfall,
dressed in white, she tells
me a true story with
desert islands and
princesses.

But later, in my sleep, I hear a knock on the windowpane.

I hear someone speaking to my mother in the next room. I

don't fully manage to wake up. A man has come to tell her

something. I recognize the voice of the gendarme. My eyes

stay screwed shut. And then I hear a cry. A cry that is very

long and very low, a cry that is partly stifled.

But I cannot tell whether I'm dreaming or if it's real.

The following day, it's clear that nothing will ever

be like before. There's a blue envelope in the kitchen.

I cannot meet my mother's eye, and she retreats when I

go near her. She talks quickly, and her head is lowered.

I already have on my wool bonnet and my coat. I look at her.

She is fretting, as if she were late, yet she does nothing.

She picks up the envelope as she passes and makes it

disappear. She rolls the wedding dress into a ball and stuffs it back on top of the wardrobe. She offers me her hand, and takes me outside, her face hidden in her shawl. The snow is already melting. It will be muddy in the school yard.

For a month I have lived in the memory of that night after the snow. My mother still cannot bring herself to look at me. She has changed. When she drops me off at school in the morning, I'm almost relieved to see her go. She walks off, shuffling, even though the ground is no longer at all slippery.

I must act quickly. *We're counting on you, Captain.* I prepare everything so I'm ready when my day comes.

✶ ✶ ✶

And finally that day does come. It is a sunny morning in
February. At the back of the class, I make every effort
to follow the chalk across the blackboard. Nothing gets
past me. Every movement of the teacher's hand. He turns
around, shaking the white dust from his sleeve.

I look again at the board. For the first time, it all
becomes clear. Like a fog that suddenly lifts, making
everything appear. My mission is nearly complete.

I must not wait any longer. This is the moment.
I am ready. I think of the medal I saw in my dream.
It all becomes possible.
Now I must fight out in
the open.

"Young lady?"

The teacher is in front of me. I had not even realized that my hand was raised. It's the first time. I've never asked anything until now.

I explain that I left my notebook at home. I want to go get it. The teacher says that's not possible.

I look at him seriously. I sit up very straight, my eyes trained on him.

"It's just at the end of the road. I know the way."

"You can use a sheet of paper."

"I need my notebook."

"No. You are staying here."

His tone is final.

I bring out my second weapon before he has time to turn away. My gaze suddenly drops to my shoes. And there is already a tear forming between my eyelashes.

This time, the blow seems to find its target. Panic in the enemy ranks. The lines cannot hold for much longer when faced with a crying little girl. But I need reinforcements.

A voice rings out beside me.

"I can go with her."

It's Edgar. He seems so well behaved that I hardly recognize him.

The teacher hesitates. I wipe away my tears with my fist. He nervously rubs his hand, still covered in chalk,

on the pocket of his coat.

"Very well."

He looks at me. Then Edgar. Then back at me.

"You have ten minutes. I don't like it when students
take off like this."

I walk down the street with my lieutenant behind me.
The village is deserted. Wet rooftops shine beneath a
cold sun. Smoke drifts from the chimney of the bakery. What
is there to show that a war is going on? The fighting is
so far from us. There are birds playing around the church's
bell tower. I see them skimming past the chimes.

Our patrol arrives in front of the house.

"Here we are."

"Is it open?" Edgar asks.

I take the key from its hiding place in the lizard's hole, to the left of the door. I'm not even scared of the lizard. I hand the key to Edgar.

"Open it, please."

The lock is old, and usually the key doesn't turn. But Edgar opens the door easily. I point to the large stone for him to sit on.

"Wait for me. I won't be long."

He crouches next to the stone. He's my best soldier.

When I enter the house, I feel that in that one instant, I have grown up. I have never been in here by myself. I take a first step. There are only two rooms:

my bedroom, which used to be my parents' when I
was much younger, and the kitchen. That's
where my mother has slept since the war.

I push open the kitchen door. I feel as
though all the objects are looking at me. Even
the clock is wondering what I'm doing there.

But still I pull a chair toward the shelves.
It groans against the floor to tell me it
doesn't approve. I climb up and take hold
of the metal box, right there at the
top. I look at it in my hands.

And the miracle happens. The box speaks to me. I
have seen it so often, sitting there, mute, on the table,
with its drawings of sheep resting beneath a tree, the
shepherd in the distance. . . . This closed box starts talking.

The words come slowly.

Assorted . . . sweets.

It's written there, on one line, in violet letters.

I have been fighting that for months. It was my mission. I can read.

I get down from my chair, place the box on the table, and push open the lid. The envelopes are there.

I take the one on top. I open it. I am too breathless to follow my father's sloping handwriting, but I pick out the smallest words, those that jump toward my face as I lean over.

The word *rats,* the word *blood,* the word *fear.*

My mother never read me those words.

There's an underlined sentence that says, *The rain here is made of metal and fire.*

And lower down, as if they had collapsed to the foot of

the page, the words *buried alive* and *butchery*.

I look for the letter on which he drew the soldiers at the edge of the forest. Here it is. I unfold it. I look for the word *trout* and the word *stream,* which my mother had read out. There's no sign of any stream, any trout, any mill. Nothing.

All that is written is *At night I cry in the mud* or *Oh, my darling, you will never see me again.*

At the end I see my name. He wrote it in lovely round letters, as if it were in a different language, as if I were from a different planet.

Give Rosalie a kiss.

"What are you doing?"

Edgar's voice. I don't turn around. He must not see his captain's tears.

"You can read?" he asks.

I jam the letters back into the box. My hands are shaking as I search for the blue envelope.

"Did you learn to read?" he says again.

"I want to find my notebook."

"You hid it under your shirt. You already had it in the classroom. We have to go. They'll find us."

I put the box back on the shelf and pull out the notebook that was tucked under my shirt.

I imagine metal falling from the sky, my father lying beneath the burning rain.

As we leave the house, I feel pain, but something has

opened inside me. I stop a second. I breathe in the pure, pungent air of truth.

"Why didn't you tell the teacher that I had the notebook beneath my shirt?" I ask Edgar on the way back.

He shrugs and carries on walking ahead of me.

"Because we're on the same side."

I'm back on my bench in the classroom. I am thinking about the blue envelope. Where has it gone? It arrived the night after the snow. It knows the final secret.

There have been no letters since.

I've stopped listening to everything around me. It's the end of the morning. Lunchtime. Thinking back, I do not remember the hours that followed.

When the bell rings for recess, everyone rushes to grab

their coats. I stay there, sitting through the storm.

"Are you coming?" I hear Edgar ask. I do not move. Some of the students start going out to the school yard.

"If they come looking for me," I say to Edgar, "tell them I went to the stream, up by the mill."

He studies me. The commotion continues around us.

"Do you need me?"

"I need you to tell them that I went to the stream. Okay?"

He stands down.

I slip off the bench and curl into a ball. The teacher stamps his foot at the door.

"Get a move on! Outside."

He is already stuffing his pipe with tobacco.

"Edgar!" he yells. "I'm about to shut the door."

Edgar files out. I stay hidden under my bench.

The door slams. I can
hear my breathing in the
deserted room. After a few
seconds, I slide toward the
window, the one that faces
the street. I open it.

I pause for a moment. The sweet smell of the pipe is
coming around from the school yard, along with the cries
of the children.

Eventually I scale the window and jump out onto
the street. I don't take the direction of the stream.
I run home.

I grab the key from the lizard's hole. For the first time,
I manage to open the door. The box. The letters spread
across the kitchen table. The blue envelope is not there.

I stand up. I look in the saucepans, the drawers, the cabinet by the front door, the wardrobe. I search the pockets of my mother's clothes and among the papers in the big red file. Where is the letter? I no longer know what I'm doing. I look under the mattress, between the slats of the bed. I unmake up my mother's bed. The sheets lie strewn around the room like ghosts. And then, suddenly, I look up at the top of the wardrobe. The wedding dress, rolled up in a bundle. I climb onto the stove just next to it. I lift up the dusty cloth. I cannot see a thing as I run my hand underneath.

It's there. Under the lace of the veil.
I take the square blue envelope.

I go and sit down at the table. I open it.

Ministry of War.

These three words written at the top.
I only read the ones that come to me.

Madame, regret, pain, and then my
father's full name. And then seven
more words that feel like seven cannon
shots in the early evening:

Killed in action fighting for his country.

These words resound in me long into
the night. They kick up a cloud of dust.

Killed in action fighting for his country.

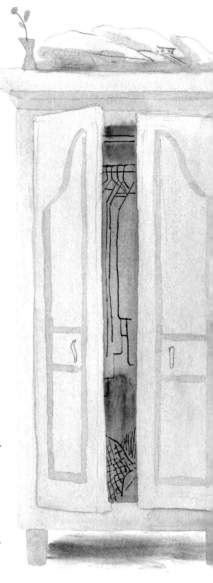

* * *

As for the rest, Edgar filled me in sometime later:

Class resumes after recess, and it takes the teacher
a moment to notice my absence. Not much different from the
sense that a piece of furniture is missing from the room.

"And the little one?"

He inspects the coat hooks, walks between the rows of desks,
and makes the students stand up as if one of them might have
sat on me or hidden me in his pocket. He looks under his desk.

"Sir, Edgar wants to say something."

And indeed Edgar is there with his hand up.

The teacher goes over to him.

"She told me something about the stream.
She told me she wanted to
go to the stream by
the mill."

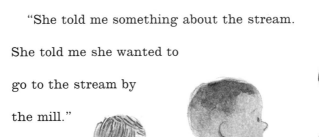

"The stream."

The teacher spins around, his face white. He seems to
be searching for an escape route.

"My God, the stream. Put on your coats."

In an instant, everyone is outside. This might have been
cause for excitement, but a deep silence reigns.
The only sound is the hammering of
soles across the schoolyard.

The teacher turns to Robert,
the gendarme's son.

"You, go and find your father."

The students set off on the double toward the stream.
It's the first time anyone has seen the teacher run.
Darkness starts to fall. Edgar leads the troops.

When they get to the bank, they see that the water
has risen. The stream is a torrent. The teacher is so
pale, he looks like a worm glistening in the shadow of
the willows.

"My God!" he murmurs. "What drove her to this?"

Edgar organizes two parties. One to go upstream,
the other down. The gendarme arrives with his son and
another policeman. They go and investigate the wheel of
the mill, which is striving to keep up with everything the
current sends its way.

"What about her mother?" asks the teacher. "What do
we tell her mother?"

A sputtering of voices can be heard here and there
along the water.

"Rosalie! Rosalie!"

"Can she swim?"

"Rosalie!"

And everyone realizes that they have never uttered my name.

It is pitch-black when my mother arrives. She stops by
the school, where a student is keeping watch. He tells her
that I have disappeared. She runs to the stream.

The teacher goes to meet her. He has
mud on his nose and in his hair.
His shoes are filled with water.

"Madame . . ."

He is unable to say
anything more.

My mother looks at the surface of the water. The gendarme is back from the mill.

"She spoke of this place to a fellow student. Did your daughter sometimes come up here?"

My mother does not answer. The gendarme takes her by the arm and draws her to one side.

"Tell me . . . is there any way that the news of her father—"

"No," says my mother, her voice weak.

"She seemed so strong. . . ."

"I didn't tell her anything about her father."

"Sorry?"

"I haven't been able to tell her. I can't. Every evening, I try to talk to her, but . . ."

She looks away.

The gendarme falls silent.

Edgar steps out of the shadows. He has heard everything.

"I just wanted to say, I think I saw Rosalie at your house through the kitchen window. The door is locked from the inside."

Now there are fifty people outside the house, waiting in the darkness. My mother goes up to the window. She presses herself against the glass.

"Rosalie . . ." It's all my mother can say. She sees me asleep amid the letters, my head on the table. The wax from the candle is melting onto the envelopes next to me.

"What's all that around her?" asks the teacher, whose forehead is resting on the windowpane.

"She can read," says Edgar, swelling with pride.

The teacher turns to him, lost.

"What did you say?"

"She can read, sir!"

"My God," he gasps.

A dull sound. The gendarme has just forced the door.

He does not want to be the first to go in.

He calls out to my mother.

She leaves the window, moving toward

him. The students form a guard of honor

to make way for her.

She goes in, alone, slowly.

I open my eyes. The flame of the

candle makes the kitchen look

like it's been painted gold.

I see my mother.

I sit up straight in my chair.

Her face is how I like it. The way it

is on the difficult days. She stays

on her feet, by the table.

"I wanted to know," I say.

"Yes, Rosalie."

"And now I do."

"Yes."

She steps forward and

takes me in her arms, and I cry with her.

The gendarme disperses the little crowd by the door.

Bright dots vanish into the night.

My mother takes a blue parcel from her pocket.

It is thicker, a package with the words *Ministry of War*

that she has already opened.

"This came today. It's for you."

I open the package. First there's a letter. I make out the words *Died for his country* that I already know. And then some words I don't know, like *posthumously* and *grateful compatriots*. But inside the package, underneath the letter, sits a heavy object in a small velvet bag.

I turn toward the window.

Edgar is outside, looking at me. I smile at him through my tears.

"It's for you," says my mother again.

I open the bag on the table.

It's a medal made of sparkling bronze with a striped ribbon.

Like a little fish, alive in my hands.